Dogerella

by Maribeth Boelts
illustrated by Donald Wu

Random House 🏠 New York

Once upon a time,

there was a mean stepdog-mother

and two stepdog-sisters.

Dogerella was their servant.

"Dogerella! Fetch my chew toy!"
said one stepdog-sister.

"Dogerella! Scratch my fleas!"
said the other stepdog-sister.

"Dogerella! Fluff my tail!"
said the stepdog-mother.

At night, Dogerella curled up
by the fire.
She dreamed of a home
where she was loved.

Princess Bea lived in a palace.

For her fifth birthday,

she was given rubies.

For her sixth birthday,

she was given

rings and roses.

It would soon be
her seventh birthday.
Princess Bea did not want
rubies, rings, or roses.
She wanted a dog.

The queen fussed.

She told Princess Bea

that dogs were too silly.

They were too furry.

They went

to the bathroom outside!

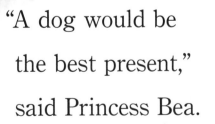

"A dog would be
the best present,"
said Princess Bea.

Then the king had an idea.

They would throw a ball

for all the dogs in the kingdom.

Princess Bea would choose
the finest dog for her pet.
That dog would get
a golden bone.

The royal page

went door to door.

He invited all the dogs

to the ball.

"Can I go, too?"

asked Dogerella.

"Of course not,"

said her stepdog-mother.

She ordered Dogerella

to help them get ready.

Dogerella fluffed
their tangled tails.

She clipped
their yellow toenails.

She freshened
their doggy breath.

16

When they left for the ball,

Dogerella cried.

How she wished she could go!

Just then,

Dogerella's Fairy Dogmother

appeared.

She could make

Dogerella's wishes come true.

She waved her wand

over Dogerella's head.

"*Meow,*" said Dogerella.

She waved her wand again.

"Hee-haw," said Dogerella.

The Fairy Dogmother

put new batteries into her wand.

She waved it one last time.

Dogerella was turned back
into herself.
But she did have
a sparkly new collar.

There was no time to waste.
The Fairy Dogmother
clicked her paws
over a dog biscuit.

It turned into a mini-van.

Dogerella jumped in.

The mini-van raced to the palace.

At the palace,
Dogerella's heart pounded.

Some dogs wore crowns.
Some dogs had
broad chests and deep barks.
Some dogs had pink toenails
and extra-fluffy tails.
All the dogs looked their best.

Dogerella crawled
up the palace steps.
"Stop!" a guard shouted.
"A mutt like you
can't come to the ball!"

The guard put Dogerella
on a chain in the royal backyard.

Dogerella peeked
into a palace window.
She watched dogs
prance and dance
and do clever tricks.

But they also snapped
and snarled.
They stole
each other's royal treats, too.

The king patted
the best hunting dogs.
The queen petted
the prettiest dogs.

Princess Bea turned away.
She tried not to cry.
"I just want a dog
who is my *friend*,"
she said.

The king and queen

did not hear her.

But Dogerella did!

Her ears stood straight up.

She could be a friend

to Princess Bea!

Princess Bea left the ball.

She plopped down by the pond

in the royal backyard.

In the dark,

Dogerella wagged her tail.

She whimpered.

Princess Bea threw

the golden bone into the water.

Splash!

Dogerella pulled at the chain
around her neck.
She pulled so hard
her sparkly collar popped off!

She ran to the pond
and jumped in the water.

She paddled to the golden bone
and scooped it up.

"Here, dog!"

laughed Princess Bea.

Dogerella wagged her whole body

and dropped the bone.

"Good girl!" said Princess Bea.

Dogerella wiggled with joy.

Princess Bea

threw the bone again.

Dogerella brought it back.

Then she chased her tail.

She gave Princess Bea
her paw to shake.

Princess Bea picked up

the sparkly collar in the grass.

Whose was it?

Dogerella's mean stepdog-sisters
dashed from the palace.
They knocked into Princess Bea.
They barked and jumped.

Princess Bea tried the collar
on the first stepdog-sister.
It was too tight.

She tried it
on the second stepdog-sister.
It was too big.

She tried it on Dogerella.

It fit just right!

Princess Bea gave Dogerella
a hug.

Dogerella licked her cheek.

In the palace,

Princess Bea told everyone

the good news.

Dogerella would get

the golden bone.

She would be the royal pet.

She tried it on Dogerella.

It fit just right!

Princess Bea gave Dogerella
a hug.

Dogerella licked her cheek.

In the palace,
Princess Bea told everyone
the good news.
Dogerella would get
the golden bone.
She would be the royal pet.

The other dogs

stomped their paws.

They growled and howled.

They nipped and yipped.

"The ball is over,"

said Princess Bea.

But none of the dogs would leave.

"What will we do?"

asked Princess Bea.

Suddenly,

the Fairy Dogmother came to help.

She waved her wand.

A carriage
filled with cats appeared.
Dogs chased cats
out of the palace
and into the woods.

"That's much better,"
said Princess Bea.
"Now we can live
happily ever after . . .
together!"

"Woof!" said Dogerella.